THE TAILOR OF GLOSTER

SQUIRREL NUTKIN

TOM KITTEN

PETER RABBIT

THE TALE OF
THE PIE AND
THE PATTY-PAN

FOR JOAN, TO READ TO BABY

BUTTER AND MILK FROM THE FARM

THE TALE OF
THE PIE AND
THE PATTY-PAN

BY

BEATRIX POTTER

Author of
" The Tale of Peter Rabbit," &c.

Pussy-cat sits by the fire — how should she be fair ?
In walks the little dog — says " Pussy are you there ?
How do you do Mistress Pussy ? Mistress Pussy, how do you do ?"
" I thank you kindly, little dog, I fare as well as you !"
Old Rhyme.

FREDERICK WARNE

Frederick Warne has a continuing commitment to reproduce Beatrix Potter's exquisite watercolours to the highest possible standard. In 1993 and 1994, taking advantage of the latest advances in printing technology and expertise, entirely new film was made from her original book illustrations. The drawings are now reproduced with a quality and a degree of authenticity never before attainable in print.

FREDERICK WARNE

Published by the Penguin Group
27 Wrights Lane, London W8 5TZ, England
Penguin Books USA Inc., 375 Hudson Street, New York, N.Y . 10014, USA
Penguin Books Australia Ltd, Ringwood, Victoria, Australia
Penguin Books Canada Ltd, 10 Alcorn Avenue, Toronto, Ontario, Canada M4V 3B2
Penguin Books (N.Z.) Ltd, 182-190 Wairau Road, Auckland 10, New Zealand

Penguin Books Ltd, Registered Offices: Harmondsworth, Middlesex, England

First published 1905 by Frederick Warne
This edition with new reproductions of Beatrix Potter's book
illustrations first published 1995

New reproductions copyright © Frederick Warne & Co., 1995
Original copyright in text and illustrations © Frederick Warne & Co., 1905

Frederick Warne & Co. is the owner of all rights, copyrights and trademarks
in the Beatrix Potter character names and illustrations.

Colour reproduction by
Saxon Photolitho Ltd, Norwich
Printed and bound in Great Britain by
William Clowes Limited, Beccles and London

ONCE upon a time there was a Pussy-cat called Ribby, who invited a little dog called Duchess, to tea.

"Come in good time, my dear Duchess," said Ribby's letter, "and we will have something so very nice. I am baking it in a pie-dish—a pie-dish with a pink rim. You never tasted anything so good! And *you* shall eat it all! *I* will eat muffins, my dear Duchess!" wrote Ribby.

Duchess read the letter and wrote an answer:—"I will come with much pleasure at a quarter past four. But it is very strange. *I* was just going to invite you to come here, to supper, my dear Ribby, to eat something *most delicious*.

"I will come very punctually, my dear Ribby," wrote Duchess; and then at the end she added— "I hope it isn't mouse?"

And then she thought that did not look quite polite; so she scratched out "isn't mouse" and changed

THE INVITATION

it to " I hope it will be fine," and
she gave her letter to the postman.

But she thought a great deal
about Ribby's pie, and she read
Ribby's letter over and over again.

" I am dreadfully afraid it *will* be
mouse ! " said Duchess to herself—
" I really couldn't, *couldn't* eat
mouse pie. And I shall have to
eat it, because it is a party. And
my pie was going to be veal and
ham. A pink and white pie-dish !
and so is mine ; just like Ribby's
dishes ; they were both bought at
Tabitha Twitchit's."

Duchess went into her larder

and took the pie off a shelf and
looked at it.

"It is all ready to put into the
oven. Such lovely pie-crust; and
I put in a little tin patty-pan to

hold up the crust; and I made a hole in the middle with a fork to let out the steam—Oh I do wish I could eat my own pie, instead of a pie made of mouse!"

Duchess considered and considered and read Ribby's letter again—

"A pink and white pie-dish—and *you* shall eat it *all*. 'You' means me—then Ribby is not going to even taste the pie herself? A pink and white pie-dish! Ribby is sure to go out to buy the muffins. . . . . Oh what a good idea! Why shouldn't I rush along and put my pie into Ribby's oven when Ribby isn't there?"

Duchess was quite delighted with her own cleverness!

Ribby in the meantime had received Duchess's answer, and as soon as she was sure that the little dog could come—she popped *her* pie into the oven. There were two ovens, one above the other; some other knobs and handles were only ornamental and not intended to open. Ribby put the pie into the lower oven; the door was very stiff.

"The top oven bakes too quickly," said Ribby to herself. "It is a pie of the most delicate and tender mouse minced up with bacon. And I have taken out all the bones; because Duchess did nearly choke herself with a fish-bone last time I gave a party. She eats a little fast —rather big mouthfuls. But a most genteel and elegant little dog; infinitely superior company to Cousin Tabitha Twitchit."

THE PIE MADE OF MOUSE

Ribby put on some coal and swept up the hearth. Then she went out with a can to the well, for water to fill up the kettle.

Then she began to set the room in order, for it was the sitting-room as well as the kitchen. She shook the mats out at the front-door and put them straight; the hearth-rug was a rabbit-skin. She dusted the clock and the ornaments on the mantelpiece, and she polished and rubbed the tables and chairs.

Then she spread a very clean white table-cloth, and set out her best china tea-set, which she took out of a wall-cupboard near the fireplace. The tea-cups were white with a pattern of pink roses; and the dinner-plates were white and blue.

When Ribby had laid the table she took a jug and a blue and white dish, and went out down the field to the farm, to fetch milk and butter.

When she came back, she peeped into the bottom oven; the pie looked very comfortable.

Ribby put on her shawl and bonnet and went out again with a basket, to the village shop to buy a packet of tea, a pound of lump sugar, and a pot of marmalade.

And just at the same time, Duchess came out of *her* house, at the other end of the village.

Ribby met Duchess half-way down the street, also carrying a basket, covered with a cloth. They only bowed to one another; they

THE VEAL AND HAM PIE

did not speak, because they were
going to have a party.

As soon as Duchess had got
round the corner out of sight—she
simply ran! Straight away to
Ribby's house!

Ribby went into the shop and

bought what she required, and
came out, after a pleasant gossip
with Cousin Tabitha Twitchit.

Cousin Tabitha was disdainful
afterwards in conversation—

"A little *dog* indeed! Just as if
there were no CATS in Sawrey!

And a *pie* for afternoon tea! The very idea!" said Cousin Tabitha Twitchit.

Ribby went on to Timothy Baker's and bought the muffins. Then she went home.

There seemed to be a sort of scuffling noise in the back passage, as she was coming in at the front door.

"I trust that is not that Pie : the spoons are locked up, however," said Ribby.

But there was nobody there. Ribby opened the bottom oven door with some difficulty, and turned the pie. There began to be

WHERE IS THE PIE MADE OF MOUSE?

a pleasing smell of baked mouse!

Duchess in the meantime, had slipped out at the back door.

"It is a very odd thing that Ribby's pie was *not* in the oven when I put mine in! And I can't find it anywhere; I have looked all over the house. I put *my* pie into a nice hot oven at the top. I could not turn any of the other handles; I think that they are all shams," said Duchess, "but I wish I could have removed the pie made of mouse! I cannot think what she has done with it? I heard Ribby coming and I had to run out by the back door!"

Duchess went home and brushed
her beautiful black coat ; and then
she picked a bunch of flowers in
her garden as a present for Ribby ;
and passed the time until the clock
struck four.

Ribby—having assured herself by careful search that there was really no one hiding in the cupboard or in the larder—went upstairs to change her dress.

She put on a lilac silk gown, for the party, and an embroidered muslin apron and tippet.

"It is very strange," said Ribby, "I did not *think* I left that drawer pulled out; has somebody been trying on my mittens?"

She came downstairs again, and made the tea, and put the teapot on the hob. She peeped again into the *bottom* oven, the pie had become a lovely brown, and it was steaming hot.

READY FOR THE PARTY

She sat down before the fire to wait for the little dog. "I am glad I used the *bottom* oven," said Ribby, "the top one would certainly have been very much too hot. I wonder why that cupboard door was open? Can there really have been some-one in the house?"

Very punctually at four o'clock, Duchess started to go to the party. She ran so fast through the village that she was too early, and she had to wait a little while in the lane that leads down to Ribby's house.

"I wonder if Ribby has taken *my* pie out of the oven yet?" said

Duchess, "and whatever can have become of the other pie made of mouse?"

At a quarter past four to the minute, there came a most genteel little tap-tappity. "Is Mrs. Ribston at home?" inquired Duchess in the porch.

"Come in! and how do you do, my dear Duchess?" cried Ribby. "I hope I see you well?"

"Quite well, I thank you, and how do *you* do, my dear Ribby?" said Duchess. "I've brought you some flowers; what a delicious smell of pie!"

DUCHESS IN THE PORCH

"Oh, what lovely flowers! Yes,
it is mouse and bacon!"

"Do not talk about food, my
dear Ribby," said Duchess; "what
a lovely white tea-cloth! . . . . Is it
done to a turn? Is it still in the
oven?"

"I think it wants another five
minutes," said Ribby. "Just a
shade longer; I will pour out the
tea, while we wait. Do you take
sugar, my dear Duchess?"

"Oh yes, please! my dear
Ribby; and may I have a lump
upon my nose?"

"With pleasure, my dear Duchess; how beautifully you beg! Oh,

how sweetly pretty!"

Duchess sat up with the sugar
on her nose and sniffed—

"How good that pie smells! I
do love veal and ham—I mean to
say mouse and bacon——"

She dropped the sugar in confusion, and had to go hunting under the tea-table, so did not see which oven Ribby opened in order to get out the pie.

Ribby set the pie upon the table; there was a very savoury smell.

Duchess came out from under the table-cloth munching sugar, and sat up on a chair.

"I will first cut the pie for you; I am going to have muffin and marmalade," said Ribby.

"Do you really prefer muffin? Mind the patty-pan!"

"I beg your pardon?" said Ribby.

"May I pass you the marmalade?" said Duchess hurriedly.

The pie proved extremely toothsome, and the muffins light and hot. They disappeared rapidly, especially the pie!

"I think"—(thought the Duchess to herself)—"I *think* it would be wiser if I helped myself to pie; though Ribby did not seem to notice anything when she was cutting it. What very small fine pieces it has cooked into! I did not remember that I had minced it up so fine; I suppose this is a quicker oven than my own."

"How fast Duchess is eating!" thought Ribby to herself, as she buttered her fifth muffin.

The pie-dish was emptying rapidly! Duchess had had four helps already, and was fumbling with the spoon.

"A little more bacon, my dear Duchess?" said Ribby.

"Thank you, my dear Ribby; I

WHERE IS THE PATTY-PAN ?

was only feeling for the patty-pan."

"The patty-pan? my dear Duchess?"

"The patty-pan that held up the pie-crust," said Duchess, blushing under her black coat.

"Oh, I didn't put one in, my dear Duchess," said Ribby; "I don't think that it is necessary in pies made of mouse."

Duchess fumbled with the spoon —"I can't find it!" she said anxiously.

"There isn't a patty-pan," said Ribby, looking perplexed.

"Yes, indeed, my dear Ribby;

where can it have gone to?" said
Duchess.

"There most certainly is not one,
my dear Duchess. I disapprove of
tin articles in puddings and pies. It
is most undesirable — (especially
when people swallow in lumps!)"
she added in a lower voice.

Duchess looked very much

alarmed, and continued to scoop the inside of the pie-dish.

"My Great-aunt Squintina (grandmother of Cousin Tabitha Twitchit)—died of a thimble in a Christmas plum-pudding. *I* never put any article of metal in *my* puddings or pies."

Duchess looked aghast, and tilted up the pie-dish.

"I have only four patty-pans, and they are all in the cupboard."

Duchess set up a howl.

"I shall die! I shall die! I have swallowed a patty-pan! Oh, my dear Ribby, I do feel so ill!"

"It is impossible, my dear Duchess; there was not a patty-pan."

Duchess moaned and whined and rocked herself about.

"Oh I feel so dreadful, I have swallowed a patty-pan!"

"There was *nothing* in the pie," said Ribby severely.

"Yes there *was*, my dear Ribby, I am sure I have swallowed it!"

"Let me prop you up with a pillow, my dear Duchess; where do you think you feel it?"

"Oh I do feel so ill *all over* me, my dear Ribby; I have swallowed

a large tin patty-pan with a sharp
scalloped edge!"

"Shall I run for the doctor? I
will just lock up the spoons!"

"Oh yes, yes! fetch Dr. Maggotty, my dear Ribby: he is a Pie

himself, he will certainly understand."

Ribby settled Duchess in an armchair before the fire, and went out and hurried to the village to look for the doctor.

She found him at the smithy.

He was occupied in putting rusty nails into a bottle of ink, which he had obtained at the post office.

"Gammon? ha! HA!" said he, with his head on one side.

Ribby explained that her guest had swallowed a patty-pan.

"Spinach? ha! HA!" said he, and accompanied her with alacrity.

DR. MAGGOTTY'S MIXTURE

He hopped so fast that Ribby had to run. It was most conspicuous. All the village could see that Ribby was fetching the doctor.

"I *knew* they would over-eat themselves!" said Cousin Tabitha Twitchit.

But while Ribby had been hunting for the doctor—a curious thing had happened to Duchess, who had been left by herself, sitting before the fire, sighing and groaning and feeling very unhappy.

"How *could* I have swallowed it! such a large thing as a patty-pan!"

She got up and went to the table, and felt inside the pie-dish again with a spoon.

51

"No ; there is no patty-pan, and I put one in ; and nobody has eaten pie except me, so I must have swallowed it !"

She sat down again, and stared mournfully at the grate. The fire crackled and danced, and something sizz-z-zled !

Duchess started! She opened the door of the *top* oven;—out came a rich steamy flavour of veal and ham, and there stood a fine brown pie,—and through a hole in the top of the pie-crust there was a glimpse of a little tin patty-pan!

Duchess drew a long breath—

"Then I must have been eating MOUSE! . . . No wonder I feel ill . . . . But perhaps I should feel worse if I had really swallowed a patty-pan!" Duchess reflected—"What a very awkward thing to have to explain to Ribby! I think I will put *my* pie in the back-yard

and say nothing about it. When
I go home, I will run round and
take it away." She put it outside
the back-door, and sat down again
by the fire, and shut her eyes; when
Ribby arrived with the doctor, she
seemed fast asleep.

"Gammon, ha, HA?" said the
doctor.

"I am feeling very much better," said Duchess, waking up with a jump.

"I am truly glad to hear it! He has brought you a pill, my dear Duchess!"

"I think I should feel *quite* well if he only felt my pulse," said Duchess, backing away from the magpie, who sidled up with something in his beak.

"It is only a bread pill, you had much better take it; drink a little milk, my dear Duchess!"

"Gammon? Gammon?" said the doctor, while Duchess coughed and choked.

"Don't say that again!" said Ribby, losing her temper—"Here, take this bread and jam, and get out into the yard!"

"Gammon and Spinach! ha ha HA!" shouted Dr. Maggotty triumphantly outside the back door.

"I am feeling very much better my dear Ribby," said Duchess. "Do you not think that I had better go home before it gets dark?"

"Perhaps it might be wise, my dear Duchess. I will lend you a nice warm shawl, and you shall take my arm."

"I would not trouble you for worlds ; I feel wonderfully better. One pill of Dr. Maggotty——"

"Indeed it is most admirable, if it has cured you of a patty-pan ! I will call directly after breakfast to ask how you have slept."

Ribby and Duchess said good-bye affectionately, and Duchess started home. Half-way up the lane she stopped and looked back ; Ribby had gone in and shut her door. Duchess slipped through the fence, and ran round to the back of Ribby's house, and peeped into the yard.

Upon the roof of the pig-stye sat Dr. Maggotty and three jackdaws. The jackdaws were eating pie-crust, and the magpie was drinking gravy out of a patty-pan.

"Gammon, ha, HA!" he shouted when he saw Duchess's little black nose peeping round the corner.

Duchess ran home feeling uncommonly silly!

When Ribby came out for a pailful of water to wash up the tea-things, she found a pink and white pie-dish lying smashed in the

SO THERE REALLY *WAS* A PATTY-PAN

middle of the yard. The patty-pan was under the pump, where Dr. Maggotty had considerately left it.

Ribby stared with amazement— "Did you ever see the like! so there really *was* a patty-pan? . . . . But *my* patty-pans are all in the kitchen cupboard. Well I never did! . . . . Next time I want to give a party— I will invite Cousin Tabitha Twitchit!"